Postman Pat
and the Christmas Puddings

Story by **John Cunliffe**
Pictures by **Joan Hickson**

From the original Television designs by **Ivor Wood**

André Deutsch/Hippo Books

Published simultaneously in hardback by
André Deutsch Limited
105-106 Great Russell Street, London WC1B 3LJ
and in paperback by Hippo Books, Scholastic Publications Limited,
10 Earlham Street, London WC2H 9RX in 1987

ISBN 0 233 98122 5 (hardback)
ISBN 0 590 70779 5 (paperback)

Made and printed in Belgium by Proost
Typeset in Plantin by Span Graphics, London

It was a bright day in November.
At the post-office, Mrs. Goggins said,
"Ted left a message from Granny
Dryden. She's run out of sugar, and
she says would you take a two-pound
bag when you call."
"Certainly," said Pat. "I hope she's
baking something nice."
Mrs. Goggins gave Pat a bag of sugar
with the letters, and off he went.

Pat called at Greendale Farm with
two letters and a parcel.
But Mrs. Pottage was busy.
She was very busy.
She said, "Put them on the dresser,
Pat. We're too busy to open them
just now."

The cooker was on.

Pans boiled on the hob.

The scales were out.

The mixing bowls were out.

The recipe book was open.

The table was full.

There were bags of flour, and sugar,

and raisins, and currants.

There were packets of dates, and peel,

and ground almonds.

There was a bowl of butter warming by the stove.

There was a bowl of brown eggs.

There was a small bottle of brandy.

Katy and Tom were helping.

They weighed the flour.

They beat the eggs.

They held the big wooden spoons, and stirred round and round in the big mixing bowls.

"My goodness," said Pat, "that smells good. Is it for a party?"

"No, it's for Christmas," said Katy.

"It's our Christmas pud," said Tom.

"Pudding," said Mrs. Pottage.

"And cake," said Katy.

"Lovely," said Pat, as he helped with an extra stir. "But what's that small bowl for?"

"That's your pudding," said Tom.

"Oh, it was a secret," said Katy.

"Never mind," said Pat, "I'll forget it before Christmas comes."

Mrs. Pottage put the puddings on to boil.

Tom scraped a bowl.

Katy licked a wooden spoon. She gave Pat the other one. They gave baby Paul a bowl to scrape, but he put it on his head!

Pat went on his way.

"Now, Jess," he said, "don't let me forget Granny Dryden's sugar."

Pat called next on the Reverend Timms.

The Reverend was in the kitchen, too, with lots of pans boiling and steaming.

"Are you busy with Christmas puddings as well?" said Pat.

"Bless you, no," said the Reverend.
"Miss Hubbard always makes me a
lovely one. I could never eat two. No,
I'm making grapefruit marmalade.
Always comes in handy for church
events, you know. Do have a jar for
Christmas. It goes nicely on toast."
"Thank you very much," said Pat.

Pat was on his way.

At Thompson Ground, Alf was busy icing the Christmas cake.

"He does it better than me," said Dorothy.

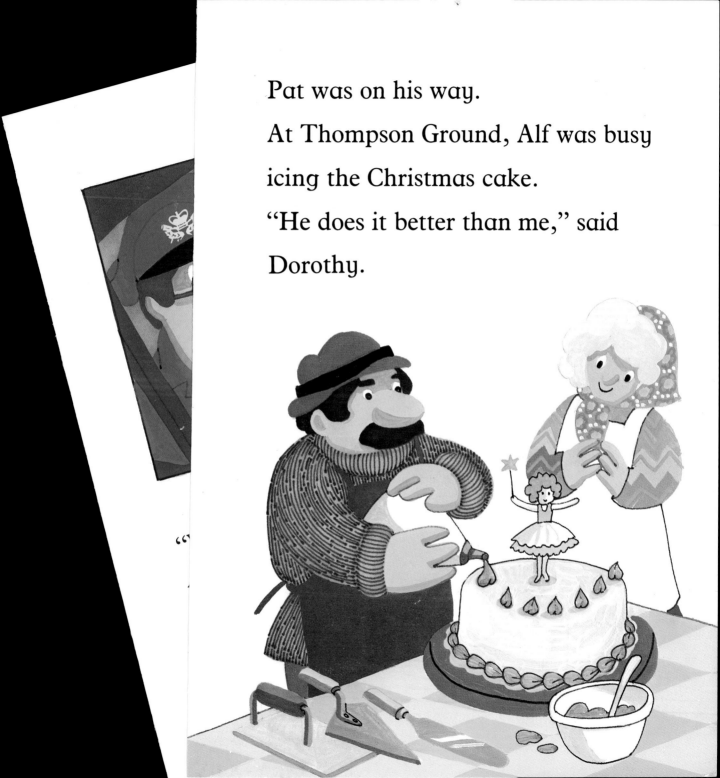

Dorothy h
puddings
Pat.
"Than
his wc

Granny Dryden was always glad to see Pat, but she was specially glad to see him today.

"Did you bring the sugar?" was the first thing she said.

"Yes, I've brought it," said Pat. "It's been cakes and puddings all the way. It would have been hard to forget."

"Oh, that's lovely," said Granny Dryden. "You are a dear. I'll make you an extra pudding as a special 'thank you'."

"That's er . . . very kind of you," said Pat, wondering how many puddings that would make.

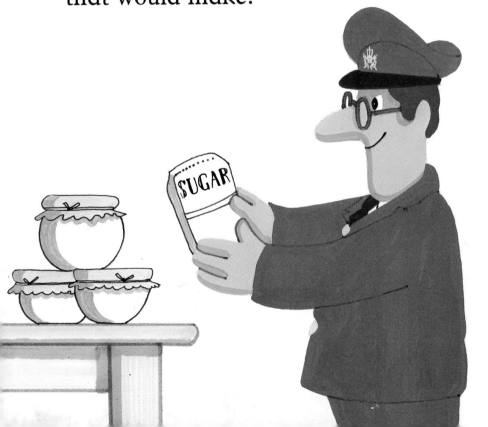

Even Ted was busy in the kitchen when Pat called.

He had a big machine on the table.

It was whizzing and whirring like a
cement-mixer.

"Whatever is that?" said Pat.

"It's the Doctor's food-mixer," said
Ted. "I've been putting a new motor
in it. I'm trying it out on my mum's
favourite recipe for . . ."

"I can guess," said Pat. "Don't tell
me . . . I bet it's for Christmas
pudding."

"You're right!" said Ted. "How did
you guess?"

"I can see into the future," said Pat.

"There's just one catch," said Ted.

"You see, it's a big mixer, and it only works with large amounts. I think I've mixed enough for about ten Christmas puddings."

"Oh dear," said Pat.

"Anyway, I'll keep three for you. You'll easily manage three, won't you?"

"Well," said Pat, "I can't . . ."

"I know you like Christmas pudding," said Ted, "so don't be shy about having three. They'll be gone in no time."

And Pat didn't have the heart to say "No".

When Pat called on Miss Hubbard he was glad to see that she was busy making blackberry wine. There were no puddings in sight. When she said, "I've kept a special bottle of Christmas wine for you, Pat," he was really pleased.

BLACCK
BERRRy
NOOV

But when she opened the cupboard
and took out a fat round packet, and
said, "And a real home-made pudding
to go with it," poor Pat almost
fainted.

He said, in a wobbly voice,
"Th...thank y...you very much, Miss
H-H-Hubbard."

By the end of the week, Pat had collected ten Christmas puddings in the back of his van.

"Oh, Jess," he said, "all these puddings! They're just too much for me. I don't think I could eat even one now."

I don't know what would have happened to all those puddings if Pat hadn't had a broken spring on the van.

He had to take his van into Pencaster to get it mended.

He did some Christmas shopping
whilst he waited for it. There was a
Christmas tree in the market-place.
Some people were collecting for
homeless families.

Pat put some money in the collecting
box, and the man said, "Thanks.
That'll be a good help for the
Christmas Dinner."

"Did you say Christmas Dinner?"
said Pat. "Is that what you're
collecting for?"

"It certainly is," said the man.

"Would you like some lovely home-
made puddings?" said Pat. "Ten of
them?"

"Great!" said the man. "Just what we
need. Great! Thanks!"

In the end, Pat put his name down to help with the dinner.

Everyone loved the puddings, and ate them up to the last morsel.

When Christmas was over, and Pat's friends said, "And how was the pudding?" Pat could truly say, "Delicious! Really delicious."
I wonder if he'll get ten next year?